Babysitting for
BENJAMIN

by Valiska Gregory

Illustrated by Lynn Munsinger

Little, Brown and Company
Boston   Toronto   London

For Melissa,
whose lop it was;
and for Holly,
who knocked on her door
  — V. G.

For Lindsey
  — L. M.

With thanks for support from the Butler University
Writers' Studio — Department of English
  — V. G.

First Edition

Library of Congress Cataloging-in-Publication Data

Gregory, Valiska.
    Babysitting for Benjamin / by Valiska Gregory ; illustrated by Lynn Munsinger. — 1st ed.
      p. cm.
    Summary: An elderly couple's well-ordered house is turned upside down when they agree to babysit a messy toddler.
    ISBN 0-316-32785-9
    [1. Babysitter — Fiction. 2. Orderliness — Fiction.]
    I. Munsinger, Lynn, ill. II. Title.
    PZ7.G8624Bab   1993
    [E] — dc20   92-18373

10 9 8 7 6 5 4 3 2 1

NIL

Published simultaneously in Canada
by Little, Brown & Company (Canada) Limited

Printed in Italy

When Benjamin knocked on the door, Frances put the goldfish on a high shelf, the lamp shade in the basement, and the pencils in the closet.

"His father said he eats pencils," said Frances.

"I know," said Ralph, twirling his whiskers nervously.

Ralph took down the pictures, rolled up the rug, and put a gate in front of the stairs.

"Of course, he's just a baby," said Frances.

"I know, dear," said Ralph. "But he's already much bigger than we were at his age, and we need to be prepared."

"Are you ready?" asked Frances.

"Ready," said Ralph, and he slowly opened the door.

"PLAY!" shouted Benjamin, sliding through the living room on his
back feet.

"I thought he would hippity-hop," said Ralph.

"No, dear," said Frances. "His mother said he leaps."

Benjamin took a large bite out of a Boston fern and jumped up and down on the sofa. Ralph put the fern on the back porch, and Frances handed Benjamin a carrot.

"EAT!" shouted Benjamin, and he snapped the carrot in two with his huge baby teeth.

"He doesn't nibble," said Frances.

"No, dear," said Ralph. "His father said he chews — on everything."

Benjamin grinned and flopped his lop ears once to the right and once to the left.

"Look, Ralph," said Frances. "He's smiling."

"I know," said Ralph. "Be careful."

It was a long afternoon. Benjamin chewed on the sofa, knocked
over the gate, and leaped into the garbage.

"PLAY!" he shouted happily, squashing an empty milk carton.
"EAT!" he said as Frances deftly removed a washcloth from his
mouth.

Ralph and Frances were exhausted by the time Benjamin's parents came to get him at the end of the day.

"I'll say this for him," said Ralph. "He sure is lively."

"Yes, dear," said Frances. "He is."

The next time Benjamin knocked on the door, Ralph taped the
telephone cord too high for chewing, and Frances put the dishes
in the attic.

"Sometimes," said Ralph, "I wonder why we're doing this."

"You remember, dear," said Frances gently. "We wanted a little
company."

Ralph frowned. "I think we got a *lot* more company than we
bargained for."

"Do you have the peanuts ready?" asked Frances.

"Ready," said Ralph, holding up a wooden bowl. Frances took a deep breath and opened the door.

"PLAY!" shouted Benjamin, whizzing through the door. He
stopped suddenly and lifted his nose in the air. Just as if he were a toy
on a string, he rolled over to the bowl in Ralph's hand.

"DUMP!" he shouted cheerfully and thumped the bowl with his huge baby foot. The bowl flew as high as the ceiling, and peanuts poured down like rain. Benjamin's nose twitched as he ate.

"Oh, Ralph," said Frances, sighing, "I think he's learned a new word!"

"I know," said Ralph. "It's too bad he couldn't have learned a word like *sleep*."

Before Benjamin left that afternoon, he had eaten every single peanut. He had also dumped the garbage, dumped the umbrella stand, and dumped three shelves of books from the bookcase. He had even dumped the can that held Ralph's collection of antique marbles.

"I hope you don't lose your marbles," said Frances.

"You can say that again," said Ralph.

"Next time," said Frances firmly, "we'll have to be better prepared."

But the next time Benjamin came over, he forgot to knock.

"PLAY!" said Benjamin, slamming the door behind him.

Ralph and Frances ran around the room in circles. "Get the pencils!" shouted Frances. She put the plants in the oven and the umbrella stand in the garbage.

"Find the peanuts!" shouted Ralph. He put the lamp shade on his head and the goldfish in the refrigerator.

Benjamin thought a minute. "PLAY!" he shouted gaily. He put Ralph and Frances in the closet.

"I think he's learned about doorknobs," whispered Frances.

"I know," said Ralph, banging on the door with his fist. "I just wish he'd learn how to play."

Frances nodded. "The problem is he likes to play with everything."

"The problem is," said Ralph, "not everything likes to play with him."

"If I were Benjamin," Frances said, "I'm not sure I'd know which was which."

Frances and Ralph stared at each other, and suddenly, they both knew exactly what they ought to do.

The next time Benjamin knocked on the door, everything was in its place. The fishbowl was on the table, the pencils were on the desk, and the garbage was in the garbage can. Ralph opened the back door and moved the sofa ten inches to the left.

"Are you ready?" asked Frances.

"I'm as ready," said Ralph, "as I'm ever going to be." And together they opened the door.

"PLAY!" shouted Benjamin. He skidded past the sofa, through
the kitchen, down the hallway, and tumbled out the back door into
the yard.

Benjamin blinked his eyes. To his right was a sandbox, and to his left was a swing. There were trees for shade and carrots in the garden just right for pulling up.

"PLAY!" he shouted. Benjamin leaped over the daisies and raced around and around the birdbath.

"I think he likes it, dear," said Ralph.

"Yes," said Frances, "I think he does."

"This is how we dump," said Frances, pouring sand from one bucket to another.

"DUMP," said Benjamin.

"And when we get hungry," said Ralph, "we have carrots to eat."

"EAT," said Benjamin happily. And near the end of the afternoon, when he had run and played and jumped as hard as he could, Benjamin stretched out on the picnic blanket, his chin flat against the ground, and quietly wiggled his nose.

"I think it's time to go in now," said Frances.

"Yes," said Ralph, "it's time."

"I have the books," said Frances.

"And I have the peanuts," said Ralph.

They sat on the sofa with Benjamin cuddled in the middle, and Frances turned to the first page. "'Once upon a time there were four little Rabbits,'" she read.

Benjamin's eyes opened wide. He nibbled the peanuts and looked carefully at every single picture on each page. And when they got to the end, Benjamin turned back to the beginning, and they read it again.

"He reads very well," said Ralph fondly.

"Yes," said Frances, smoothing Benjamin's fur, "he does."

Benjamin smiled and closed his eyes.

"READ," he mumbled as they all three fell sound asleep with everything in its place.